BOTH
PUBLISHING

Published in 2022 by BOTH Publishing.

The author asserts their moral right to be identified as the author of their work, in accordance with the Copyright, Designs and Patents Act, 1988.

A CIP catalogue record of this book is available from the British Library.

ISBN - 978-1-913603-18-2
eBook available - ISBN -978-1-913603-19-9

Printed by Ingram Spark.
Distributed by BOTH Publishing.

Cover design by Alistair Sims and Chrissey Harrison. Viking Ship illustration by rob zs and additional illustrations by Daler and perori licensed via Shutterstock.
Typeset by Chrissey Harrison.

Part of the Dyslexic Friendly Quick Reads Project.

www.booksonthehill.co.uk

BLOOD TOLL

For David, a fellow lover of crime :)

Snorri Kristjansson

Snorri Kristjansson

12.10.23

Other dyslexic friendly quick read titles from BOTH publishing

Silver for Silence

Sharpe's Skirmish

Six Lights off Green Scar

The House on the Old Cliffs

Ultrasound Shadow

The Clockwork Eyeball

Anchor Point

At Midnight I Will Steal Your Soul

Sherlock Holmes and the
Four Kings of Sweden

The Man Who Would Be King

Foreword

By Peter James

Back in 2010 I wrote my first *Quick Reads* novella, *THE PERFECT MURDER*. This was written as adult fiction but with no long words, and was aimed at people who struggled in some way with literacy.

I was lucky enough to win the *Reader's Favourite Award*. At the reception, I was approached by a lady in her late 50s who was close to tears. She told me my novella was the first book she had ever read that was not written for children. For years she had been too embarrassed ever to read in public – on a beach, a park or a bus or a train – because the only stories she was able to cope with were children's books.

Looking at the dyslexic friendly books BOTH published last year I can see how the larger spacing between the words and larger print create an easy-to-read and accessible format without detracting from the narrative journey. I am excited to be part of their project as it is thanks to initiatives such as the work BOTH is doing, that the condition of dyslexia is now catered for in fiction, and people, such as the lady I met, can hold her head up and read in public, like so many other ordinary people.

Blood Toll

Helga dreamed of gods and monsters.

Her bones ached after the journey from Uppsala to Hedeby, and even in her dream-haze she could still taste the raw fear she had felt in that accursed town. It sat on her like a weight-stone, and she felt dimly like she was sinking, rising, sinking. She tried to peer into the darkness facing her, but it was thick, cold and clammy to the touch. Somewhere far, far away but still too close, she was aware of something impossibly big slithering below her, like reality shifting under her feet.

She dreamed of the Aesir and the trolls, sharp-faced elves and stinking dwarves, and winced when they approached her, their voices sounding like a memory of thunder. As they drew closer, the peals turned to idiot waves bashing on a beach, but slower, deeper, a communion of mighty sea-whales, a wind in the trees. She felt like they were talking near her, to her, but she couldn't grasp the words. She snatched at understanding and snarled in wordless frustration when it slipped her grasp – and then, finally, one of them spoke in a language she knew.

"I reckon she's dead."

"She is alive," another voice said, with authority. "She breathes."

"Maybe she's a draugr," a third voice

rumbled petulantly. "They breathe, but only in the night. My nana told me—"

"Frodi, I swear to the home gods, the sky gods and any other gods you care to mention, if you mention your rotten nana one more time I will—"

"She was a wise woman," the first voice said.

"Thank you, Kjartan," the third voice rumbled.

"She was known as Yrsa the Mad," the third voice said. "Partly because it sounded good, and mostly because she was absolutely mad." A tense silence followed. "Oh, don't sulk, you big child." There was another silence, followed by a polite cough. "Fine. Your Nana was wise." Another cough. "The most wise of all wise women. Perhaps we did just pick up a draugr."

"I think that sounds likely."

"Whatever, troll-child."

"Wrap her in furs. We'll see what's what in the morning."

Her eyelids felt heavy, and she just managed to open her eyes enough to see a starry sky, the dark shadow of a figure and something like a tree – and then she fell down again, down from Valhalla, down from the high table of the rumbling gods, down, down into a deep sleep, sinking into the sound of waves lapping against wooden boards.

Helga dreamed of gods and monsters.

And then she woke up to men shouting, and she knew that it was bad. The voices blended in a cauldron of noise, but the sound was unmistakeable.

Death was rising.

And then there was something else rising, something altogether more urgent.

She clawed herself upright, fumbled for the side of her boat, which seemed much bigger than she remembered, and threw up spectacularly, watching the bile splash into the sea below, forming a mockery of her reflection. The raven-black hair, high cheekbones and the jaw most often set in fierce determination had been swapped out for a puddle of greenish liquid. *Feels about right.* Hanging over the edge of the boat, she forced herself to think.

Big.

Too big.

Not my boat.

Ship.

I'm on a ship.

With a lot of angry men.

She opened her eyes slowly and found it to be true. She could see the sleek sides of the longship, but it was slicing no waves. It just sat there, bobbing helplessly on the water. Coughing once to clear her throat, she pushed back slowly, turned – and found that the face looking at her was… familiar.

"…Breki?" she said.

Breki looked at her, his youthful brow furrowed with concern. "You're awake."

"Yes," she whispered. "Who…?"

"You are on board the Black Wyrm, the ship of Ormar Karlsson."

Helga looked at the blond wrestler, a boy in a man's frame. "How is the hand?"

"Better," Breki said, smiling.

"You heal fast." There was something in the manner of the boy that set her at ease – something that had made her warm to him from the moment she saw him. Growing up on the farm she had often envied the children of Hildigunnur, but she'd never suspected she'd win herself a little brother this late in life.

7

"Why are they so angry?"

"We saw you last night, on a tiny little skiff that would have flipped over with Njordur's next sneeze. Ormar said to grab you, then there was a bit of shifting about, and it seems someone took the chance to stab Trygve in the chest. Five times. And now the wind is gone."

Helga listened again. "It doesn't sound like they know who did it."

"You are right," Breki said. "If I were to guess, I'd say Mad Aethelstan. Because he's—"

"...mad?"

Breki gestured to a scrawny man with a scruffy beard, who sat between two red-faced and shouting men, entirely unconcerned. He was whittling at a small plank with a stubby knife. "Apparently he takes a bite out of every man he kills." There were remains in Athelstan's beard which did not immediately refute this.

"I see. And who are his friends?" Helga whispered, gesturing to the men flanking Aethelstan.

"I think the short, beefy one is Inge, and the tall, skinny one is Skarde. They are—"

"Foster-brothers," Helga said. "Raised together. The short one was the cuckoo in the nest. The tall one is sneaky, though."

Breki looked stunned. "How did you—"

"They hate each other more than friends, but less than brothers," she said, smirking. "And once they're done shouting, they'll most likely turn their backs together and fight the world."

Breki smiled. "You are a sharp one, friend."

A loud clang cut through the shouting, and a sharp-faced man with a shock of black hair stood up.

"Ormar?" Helga whispered.

Breki nodded.

"Hold your tongues unless you want them ripped out," Ormar growled. "This is not a time for yapping. Someone on the boat cut up Trygve, and I want to know who. The gods will not grant us wind until we finish this, and I am not rowing to the Franks."

"Start with the why," Helga muttered to herself.

"Gisli," Ormar said. Next to him, a kindly-looking young man with thick, sandy-coloured hair plaited into a warrior's braid snapped to, like a well-trained dog. "When we landed, who did Trygve run with?"

The young man made to speak, but he was interrupted.

"Me." The speaker, a tall and slim man with broad shoulders and the calm of someone who has survived enough raids to get grey in his hair, sat towards the middle of the boat. "When we landed, at least."

"Kjartan," Ormar said. *He's not growling at this one,* Helga noted. "Tell me. What happened?"

The quiet shush of waves on a pebbled beach was the only sound in the night. No birds sang, no night-hunters howled. It was as if the land knew to be quiet, waiting for the crunch of wood on gravel as the longship sliced the water and caught land softly. Soft-shoed feet hit the ground running, and swift shadows disappeared silently into the night. A group of six broke away, heading for a smattering of trees at a run.

Once they'd found cover, a youthful man with a twinkle in his eye whispered, "Where to, Kjartan?"

The man next to him, a solid block of menace, hit his arm hard. "Quiet, Trygve," he growled.

"Calm down, Inge," Kjartan said.

"…boy needs to know his place," the short man rumbled.

"I know my place, uncle…" the young man replied, "…and soon I'll know yours as well."

Behind the three, quiet snickers and murmurs of approval.

"The whelp has a mouth on him." Ulrik, a shadow at the back.

"If he uses it again, I'll stop it," Inge growled.

"No mouth no scream."

"Athelstan…"

The voice at the back faded to a whisper. "No mouth no scream no mouth no scream…"

"Athelstan is right," Kjartan said at the

front, keeping his voice low but clear. "We go fast, keep quiet and follow the tree line. There is a path around the back. Our job is to get in without a sound and grab the silver while Ormar and the others start some fires and make some noise at the front. And now – stop your yapping." The command in his voice silenced all of them, except the rhythmical, breathy whisper of Aethelstan in the back.

"No mouth no scream no mouth no scream..."

Clouds drifted across the moon and shadows shifted along the tree line. The hunt was on.

The men all looked at Kjartan, but he had finished.

"So – that was it?" Ormar said.

"Last time I spoke to him," Kjartan replied.

Ormar turned to look at the man named Inge. "Sounds like you didn't like your young cousin that much after all."

"That's not right! He was my brother's son, and I've known him since he was a—"

"—which is strange, considering you all but demanded he be taken along with us."

Helga watched as the sitting man reddened. "He was my brother's son, but he was also an insolent whelp, just like my brother."

"Alfgunn didn't seem to mind," a dark-haired man said, making no attempt to hide his contempt.

The knife was out in an instant, and Inge was halfway cross the boat when an arm as thick as the boom caught him across the chest and hooked him in. "No stabbing on the boat," a log of a man rumbled. "Sorry. No more stabbing. Now leggo the blade, brother."

"THAT'S A LIE! I'LL CUT YOUR TONGUE OUT AND FEED YOUR EYES TO THE WYRM, YOU—"

A quick glance passed between the big man and Ormar, and Inge collapsed with a wheeze after a swift punch to the ribs. The big man's paw seized the knife-wrist, and with a yelp the red-faced Viking dropped his blade.

"Let him go, Frode," Skarde snarled, then glared at Knut. "You are a liar."

Knut looked back at the young man and smiled. "I know what I heard."

"It's a lie," Skarde repeated. Glancing at Ormar, he sat down. "It's a lie," he muttered to himself.

"That knife looked very clean," Breki whispered to Helga.

"Mm," she muttered.

"You're thinking something," he said.

"Maybe. I don't know yet."

"Frodi, lay him down. Make sure he doesn't hurt himself," Ormar said. "As for you, Knut–" he glanced at the dark-haired man. "You should know better."

Knut sneered. "And that limp-dick

little shit," he growled. "Shouldn't have let his brother crawl up on his wife if he couldn't take a joke about it."

Breki glanced at Helga, who raised her eyebrow a fraction. "Nice friends you've picked," she whispered under her breath.

Ormar looked at Knut for a moment longer than necessary, then turned to Kjartan. "What happened next?"

"As we agreed, I took Inge with me and sent Ulrik, Skarde —" He nodded to the lanky young man whose face had been cut into a permanent sneer. "—and Trygve to meet the others round the back gate."

"And the others were...?"

There was something almost loving about how Ulrik laid down the body of the dying man. They had been about to pick a place to scale the wall when they heard him. Moments later he had appeared on the road leading up to the thick, iron-bound gate, with the tell-tale waddle of someone with a skinful of ale in them that they needed to get rid of.

Sadly, he had picked the wrong bush to relieve himself in.

Once the body was hidden, Ulrik gestured to the men following him – long-limbed Skarde and light-footed Trygve – pointing towards the torches set by the gate, arm curving. *Don't step in the light.*

Skarde shook his head, holding up his hand. *No. Stop.*

Ulrik extended both hands, palms up. *What?*

Skarde glanced over at the wall. Four square-built men, each carrying a wrist-thick cudgel, moved into view on the top of the wall, arguing about something. Their language drifted into the darkness, sounding like the meaningless, guttural sounds of woodland animals. Skarde's hands were still up. *Wait.*

Ulrik smiled, teeth gleaming in the darkness. *Good.* He reached forward and slapped Skarde on the shoulder.

Once the guards had disappeared to wherever they went to on their rounds, Ulrik whispered, "Once we're up and over, we meet just inside the gate. There is an empty barn we can hide in."

"How do you know?" Trygve whispered.

"Came here two days ago. Scouted the place in broad daylight. Sold all my furs, too," Ulrik said, still grinning. Trygve grinned back.

"Shut up," Skarde hissed. "Now *go*!"

Skirting just round the edge of the torches until they hit the wall, the Vikings worked in harmony. Ulrik was first, bending down and forming a step with his hands just above his knee. Picking up speed, Skarde leapt and landed with his left foot in Ulrik's hands, stretching up as the man below hoisted, rising so high he got his hands on the edge of the wall, pushing – and he was up and over. Moments later, Trygve followed, watching Skarde roll away moments before he

21

himself was up on the wall. A wordless hiss from the young climber and Trygve rolled onto his stomach, stretching his hands down until he felt the contact with Ulrik at the same time as Skarde's weight was on top of him, straining and pulling to give the man below the lift he needed – and there! Ulrik's elbow cleared the edge of the wall, and Skarde was immediately off and hauling the third man up. In a heartbeat they were all lying flat on top of the wall, listening for their lives, and...

Nothing.

No barking dogs, no shouting, no alarums.

The light of the torches just about thinned the darkness, and Ulrik grinned again. This time his teeth showed a lot more wolf – and he launched himself over the other side of the wall, landing silently below.

A quick dash, and the three found themselves in the barn that Ulrik had mentioned. Sneaking in, the leader hissed – to be met by an identical hiss from the depths.

"Well met, brothers," Ulrik whispered.

"Took you long enough," the voice in the dark whispered back.

"Had to keep the kid alive," Skarde whispered. "He talks too much."

"I won't," the voice snarled.

"Calm down, Knut," Ulrik whispered.

"The only thing you'll see of me,

Knut, is my arse as I beat you to the treasure," Trygve said.

"You little—"

"You should all be quiet," a voice like rolling boulders rumbled from deeper in the shadows, and Frode stepped forward, hunched over and shoulders pulled in so he could fit into the barn.

"He has no name," Knut growled from the dark. "He can't be talking like that. I'll smash his face in with a rock."

"Told you he was a cocky bastard."

"Quiet, old man. In fact – you may speak again if you kill more men than I do. How's that?"

A hiss of whispers as three men spoke at once – then a snap to silence as footsteps approached, replaced by the soft sound of metal on leather as short blades were drawn.

"Well met, fishwives." Kjartan ducked in, followed by two others.

"We could hear you from Denmark," a nasal voice whined.

"Shut up, Magnus." Ulrik sounded irritated.

"Sorry, Kjartan," Frode rumbled. "I asked them to be quiet, but they didn't. It's the kid. He winds them up."

"Well then. Let's see if we can get the kid a chance to show if he can dance the way he talks. These huts are huddled around our main prize. Ulrik?"

"The wall is fortified and hard to attack from below. The front gate of the church is barred, and heavy oak.

There is a side door in the abbey. We go in through there, quiet-like, and find where they keep the silver. Frode – your tools?"

"Got them."

"Good. Knives only indoors. Stick with the group." Ulrik paused. "And if you see the kid get anything, count it or he won't stop running his mouth."

Kjartan's voice seemed to draw them in and pull them close. "Follow Ulrik. He knows the way. There are over a hundred monks here, and none of them will take kindly to what we want to do. Ormar's boys are going to bang the gate nice and loud in a very short while, hoping to lead them on a merry run in the dark – our job is to get in, grab the silver and get out."

As one, the Vikings rose and filed out after Kjartan, into the gloom of the sleepy village.

The silence sat on the men of the longship like a shroud of death. Ormar glared at each of them in turn. Stone-faced Kjartan and lumbering Frode, lean Skarde and scowling Inge, handsome Ulrik flanked by smug, reedy Magnus and glaring Knut. Aethelstan sat in the middle, knife snick-snicking at the wood, utterly unconcerned.

"So you went in, and decided to make it a *game*."

"It wasn't—" Ulrik began. Kjartan's

calm hand on his forearm stopped the sentence.

"It was my decision," the old man said. "They were bickering, and I thought they needed a focus. I thought it would make the boy useful – and it did. He was desperate to prove himself."

"You had Frode. You had Ulrik. And you had to resort to games?"

"Trygve was a child, or near enough. Knut and Inge were acting like children," Kjartan said calmly, ignoring the outraged sputters from Inge and the glare from Knut. "I figured since I didn't have a toy sheep with me for them to play with, I had to find another way of getting their heads out of their own arses."

"Next time, use a spear," Ormar muttered.

"But wouldn't that be painful?" Frode mused.

"Yes," Ormar replied coldly. "Now, on with this—"

"Hnnngh!" The sound emerging from Aethelstan's throat quickly changed from human, to animal, to… something else.

"Inge! Kjartan!" Ormar barked, voice cracking like a whip. "Frode! Belt!"

Helga and Breki watched as the wiry man's grip on the knife in his right hand and the stick in his left tightened, knuckles turning from pink to white, veins throbbing in his gnarly hands. Eyes rolling up, his mouth twisted and his teeth gnashed. Barking like a dog, he snapped his head this way and that – but the men were upon him.

With precision, Kjartan danced along the bottom of the boat and launched himself on Aethelstan's right wrist, clasping down with both hands. As the bearded man made to strike with his left, Inge caught the elbow and hung on for dear life, lifting up onto his tip-toes as the wiry man seemed to gain the strength of several men – which Frode already had, deftly slipping a belt half the width of a man's torso over the struggling Viking and pulling it down below both elbows, forcing the arms straight.

A quick pull at a hidden rope, and the cylinder tightened around Aethelstan, who yowled like a terrified dog, snapping at everything and everyone, but Frode's big arms were wrapped around him and the big man's head was safely tucked between the madman's shoulder blades. Kjartan and Inge eased back, breathing heavily. In his hand Kjartan held Aethelstan's whittling knife, gingerly. He laid it down at the bearded man's feet with respect.

Helga looked at Breki, eyebrows raised. The whole operation had taken no more than three breaths.

Breki whispered, "I think they've done this before."

Helga smirked. "Such wisdom, in one so young."

"I think I know, though," Breki said under his breath. "I think—"

Helga very slowly put her hand out, palm down. *Quiet.* Glancing at Breki, she gave him the most clear signals she could. *Wait.* Then she looked down, to avoid attracting attention.

Before them, the madness in Aethelstan ebbed away, to be replaced with a drained expression. He looked down at his leather harness and tried shifting his arms. "No arms," he said sadly.

"That's right, old friend," Kjartan said. Aethelstan looked up at him, a question in his eyes. "You had the darkness in you again," Kjartan continued. "And this time there weren't any convenient monks to take it out on."

"No arms," Aethelstan repeated, with

finality. He looked down at his right hand. "No arms no teeth. No teeth!" He started tensing up again. "Tooth! Tooth!"

"Oh, I left it at your feet," Kjartan said quickly. "See?"

Aethelstan looked down, and the tension building in him washed out again. He smiled, like a child. "Tired."

Frode snaked a big arm around his shoulder. "Rest, you mad bag of nuts," he rumbled. "You're as bad as my grandmother."

Aethelstan chortled and leaned into Frode's chest.

"Well done," Ormar said from his position at the helm. "Now – does anyone want to tell me that they held the blade?" A collection of sharp, cruel

and hard faces looked back at him.
"Didn't think so. Continue."

The gloom of the village had given way to
the flickering light of torches in a hallway.
The raiding party stood silently as Frode
very gently propped the door back into
the doorway. It would never close again,
but from a distance it didn't look like it
had just been forced open.

Up ahead, Ulrik gestured. *Forward.* He
continued past every closed door, all on
the right-hand side.

Without words they all followed,
keeping arm's length between them,
knives up.

The voices seemed to drift towards

them, from nowhere and everywhere. Kjartan's hand shot up and pointed. *Ulrik. Skarde. Forward. Second.* He gestured past a doorway on the left, and quick as a flash Ulrik and Skarde darted past, taking up positions on the other side. *Frode.* He pointed to the near corner, and the large Viking tucked himself in tight. *Fall back.* All the others hugged the wall, hiding behind Frode's bulk.

The babble of the monks drew closer. The first, a stocky man of middle age, was two steps into the corridor when he noticed. He drew a breath to shout, and Frode's hammer caved his face in. Shocked and startled, the second gasped at the squelch, just as Skarde grabbed him and Ulrik rammed the knife expertly into his ribcage, the other arm wrapped around the man's face.

It happened in a blink – and then there was the sound of slapping feet on stone.

Elbowing past, Knut set his feet and pelted a rock into the darkness. There was a dull crunch, a thud – and then silence.

The Vikings stood silent, the only sound being the squelch as Inge ran a knife through the first monk's ribcage once, then again for good measure.

Finally, after what felt like an eternity, Kjartan pointed down the corridor where their victims had come from. *That way*.

Pulling the two bodies into pools of shadow, the Vikings snuck down the corridor, stepping over the prone body of a man with a hole where the back of his head used to be. Around a corner, past a door with a big ring in the centre, and the tight corridor opened up – and up – and up. The roof stretched up far over their heads.

"Big house," Frode whispered.

Kjartan pointed towards the far end of the cavernous space, where the moonlight caught on a big cross. *There.*

Looking suddenly small and vulnerable, the Vikings made their way through a landscape of oddly-shaped shadows, channels of light from long, narrow windows and across a stone floor worn smooth on the path to the far end of the building.

The cross was mounted on a plinth,

standing on a two-step dais. It was easily half the size of a man, glinting dully in the dusk. To the sides were box-shaped shadows.

Aethelstan hissed through his teeth.

Quiet. Kjartan's hands were out. He gestured towards the sides of the space. *Look. Doors.*

In the silence and the dark, the sound of wood splintering was thunderous.

"Found it," Frode said, holding a cabinet door in one massive hand.

"No noise!" Kjartan growled, as quietly as possible.

"I'm tired of being quiet," Inge said.

"And I'm tired of you."

"Shut up, Skarde."

"Are you going to stand here arguing like a pile of old fish-wives?" Kjartan snarled. "Or are you going to be of use? Look at the boy!"

The Vikings all turned towards the cabinet, which was now empty. Next to it stood Trygve, and they didn't even need to see his face to tell how smug he was. "I reckon Ormar will be re-arranging the seating order on the benches after this," he said. "But don't worry. I won't tell him that his precious men with their precious names wasted time bickering."

"Shut up, you shrivelled little ball sack," Inge snapped.

"Funny that, *uncle*, because that's exactly what Alfgunn said your problem was."

"I'm going to kill him," Inge said coldly. "And it's going to happen right here, in this stupid god-house, and if anyone asks –" He grabbed the big cross and lofted it, grunting with the effort. "– it was an accident."

"You'll have to catch me first, lard-bucket," Trygve said, stepping nimbly out of range.

"*Both* of you hold still and stop your mouths or we are *all* dead," Ulrik hissed. "Put it back. Listen!"

"What?" Inge grunted as he replaced the cross.

The fair-haired warrior held out his hands, begging for silence, and pointed.

Faintly, ever so faintly, the soft sound of wood on stone. Heavy wood,

40

dragged along a floor slowly, as quietly as possible… and clunking into place.

"Doors," Kjartan snapped.."Go."

Within moments, Skarde and Magnus returned.

"Three side doors, all barred."

"Big door won't budge. I checked it."

"So we're locked in," Ulrik said. "They'll be wanting to get rid of Ormar first, then they'll come for us."

"Stuck," Frode said. "Trapped. Like a fox in a trap. Like a salmon in a—"

"Hold your half-giant mouth, you oaf," Knut snapped. "We know."

"Just making sure," Frode rumbled.

"Give me time to think," Kjartan said, squeezing his forehead with one hand.

"Just let me—"

Voices rose from outside, babbling in the foreigners" tongue.

"They sound angry about something," Ulrik said. "I know a little bit... something about... fire?"

"Has Ormar torched them?" Inge said with delight.

"I smell smoke," Frode said.

"That's what happens when you put fire to one of their shitty straw roofs," Skarde said.

"No – I mean – here. Inside."

A number of voices erupted at once, interrupted by Trygve leaping up onto the dais and nearly taking Knut's dagger in his eye for the surprise of it. "Shut it, all of you," he said, dropping his cargo

42

on the floor with a thud. "Put these on."

The Vikings shuffled in the dark, unsure.

"What—"

"I'm not—"

"You can't tell me to—"

"Do it," Kjartan commanded. "Tell them your idea, boy."

"Easy. I found some kindling – one of their books – and ripped it up and stuffed it under the big door. They think the whole thing is on fire, and will be rushing in here as soon as they have enough numbers. We put on these monk things, hood up, and hide beside the door. Door opens, they swarm in, we join the swarm and wait until someone figures out that we've made our escape until we run out with them."

"That's the stupidest—"

"Shut up, Magnus. Do you have a better plan?" The darkness hid the face Magnus pulled. "Didn't think so, and your mother was a seagull. Now – move! They'll be opening the door any minute. Give me more bags!"

"What do you want bags for?"

"Just do what he says, Skarde. He knows what he's doing. We want to spread the silver out so it doesn't rattle."

"Thank you, Kjartan. Ulrik – do you speak their stupid language?"

"A little. Why?"

"Can you say. "We're saving the cross?"

A short pause, then disbelief. "You're not thinking…"

"I was told Vikings were brave and cunning," Trygve said. "Am I wrong?"

Ulrik's teeth glinted in the darkness. "You are not. Let's save the cross. We meet by the gate. Come on!"

With increasing speed, Vikings changed into bulky, unsightly monks and gathered up against the wall by the big door. They could hear activity behind it and several raised voices – and then the grating of stone and chain. The doors creaked mightily as they swung open, and two longships" worth of men swarmed in, shouting war cries. The Vikings stepped into the flow, keeping their eyes trained on the leaders, two broad-shouldered men in mail shirts wielding well-used cudgels with practiced ease. A couple of shouted commands and the men fell in tight.

"It's all the same, isn't it?" Skarde whispered to Knut.

"You don't need language to be a fighting bastard," Knut whispered back.

Within moments the voices rose, as someone discovered the missing silver that was currently perilously wrapped inside the garments of nine very new neophytes of the order, all of whom had inched towards a position quite close to the dais. One of the big leaders gave an order, and the men started to turn towards the door.

Now! Trygve nudged Ulrik.

Moving with purpose, flanked by Frode,

Ulrik barked something at one of the leaders and got a confirmation in return. Frode yanked up the cross with ease, and carried it out easily. The other leader of the monks patted Ulrik on the back as they went, moving out through the big doors.

The starlit sky seemed like sunlight after the gloom of the church. The sounds of fighting could be heard in the distance, and a fire was sinking its teeth into the roof of a building. One of the monks belted out a command, and the fighters took off at a run in the direction of the sea.

One by one, nine novice monks took accidental wrong turns, drifted off, were overtaken or suddenly remembered their duties elsewhere.

Weaving through the terrified village, the disguised Vikings came together at a narrow turn before the side gate, stepped onto the lane – and were confronted by four big guards, clubs in hand, barring their way.

The one in the lead barked something incomprehensible.

"Ulrik?" Kjartan said. "No, actually. Never mind." With a speed that belied his age, Kjartan swung a dagger at the man's throat and opened it precisely, just below the Adam's apple, sending a spray of blood outwards and drowning his shout in a gurgle of blood. Skarde appeared like a ghost behind the men, grabbing one with a chokehold and rapidly turning his back into a sieve. Athelstan leapt on another before he'd had the chance to swing the club or shout a warning, going straight for the man's throat with his teeth. Stunned by the flurry, the last of the gate guards just had time to register Frode's size before the stolen cross came down on him and caved in his skull.

The encounter was done within five heartbeats.

Leaving the bodies sprawled, the Vikings opened the gate and vanished into the night.

"And that's it? That's all?" Ormar looked at Ulrik, as if glaring at him would somehow extract more truth.

"That is all that I am aware of," he replied, holding his captain's gaze.

"Skarde – you were next to him going out. Did he say anything to you?"

"Nothing," Skarde said.

"Kjartan?" The old warrior nodded once. "Inge?" A shrug.

"It's what happened," Frode rumbled.

"And nobody knows, and nobody saw, and nobody stabbed the boy," Ormar growled.

Silence.

"ANSWER ME!" he roared.

Nothing.

Nothing, except the flap of wings, followed by the landing of a massive and smug raven on the top of the mast.

"I didn't," Inge said. "And you know I'd happily have taught the whelp a lesson with a little bit of time."

"He attacked your name," Ormar said. "He said you were a—"

"Yes, he did," Inge snapped. "And for that he'd have gotten what he deserved. But it wasn't a knife in the night."

The ship swayed gently in the silence. Atop the mast, the raven quorked once.

"Oh, shut up," Helga muttered. Breki shot her a questioning look. *Never mind,* she mouthed.

Do you know?

…maybe.

"Look," Ulrik said. "We are all brothers of the edge. We have all risked our lives for one another. And we've all seen what you do, and I believe none of us would be stupid enough to lie to your face."

General, very cautious, mutterings of agreement from the gathered men.

"Well… almost all of us," Ulrik said, looking at Aethelstan.

This is bad, Breki mouthed to Helga, but she ignored him, staring intently at the Vikings – and one of them in particular. She shifted in her seat and reached for something by her feet.

Ormar shook his head. "No," he said flatly. "Not a chance."

"Think about it," Inge said. "Do you think he remembers one in ten of the ones he's killed?"

Aethelstan snorted. "Heh," he added, licking his lips.

The styriman's shoulders sank. "I … not on my *ship*," he muttered. "I don't believe it."

"He's as mad as a bag of rats." Frode rumbled.

"Maybe you should believe it," Ulrik said.

"But why would he?"

"You know how he gets," Inge said.

"The rage comes on him and he doesn't know where he is. He cut off Gunnar's ear back home," Magnus whined.

"Shut up, Magnus," Skarde said, almost on reflex.

Ormar sighed heavily and reached for the dagger at his belt—

May the spirit of my mother and all strong women be with me. "And maybe you shouldn't," Helga said.

She might as well have dropped a dead deer into a den of wolves. An entire longship's worth of battle-hardened Vikings turned to look at her. Ormar blinked and frowned, as if to see if she was just in his head and could be made to disappear.

When she stubbornly persisted in being alive and on his boat, the styriman turned towards her. "Who are you, and what made you think I wanted you to speak?"

Helga felt her blood run cold. *Like too many times before,* she thought, and for a moment all the times she had stared death in the face came back to her. *And yet… I am still alive.* Fear turned to a burning joy, and she very carefully rose to her feet, aided by Breki's good arm.

She looked right back at the warrior with his hand on the tiller. "My name is not as important as yours. But Aethelstan didn't do it."

"How would you know? It happened before we picked you up," Kjartan said.

"And how would you know that?" Helga replied, smiling sweetly. "The *exact* moment when it happened?"

Kjartan made to answer, then caught up with himself and eyed Helga with suspicion. He glanced up at the raven on the mast, then sat back, motioning for her to go on. She turned to Ormar, who nodded.

"You listened to their stories," she said. "And you must have known, as we all do now, that Trygve was an arrogant little shit." She scanned her audience – *there*. A twinkle in an eye, a quickly hidden smirk. They were listening. Ormar nodded again, an almost imperceptible movement. "But being a quick-thinking, risk-taking wildcat isn't enough to get you killed, or… Skarde? And Ulrik?" She picked out her targets, who looked back at her when she named them. "– would have been dead a long time ago."

There were undisguised grins all round. Inge elbowed Skarde, who hit him back. The only one that kept an eye on her was the old warrior, Kjartan, who seemed to be watching the moves rather than enjoying the game. Helga thought back on her mother, spinning yarns for the family. *Know your audience. Oh, and remember that this audience will happily slit your throat and throw you overboard.*

She kept her oar-dance going. "Inge –" She sensed their anticipation. "– I saw your anger, and I know your pain." He looked back at her, teeth gritted. She had managed to get to the position of skald and storyteller for them, so he didn't launch himself at her – but she had very little time. "You care for your name, but not half as much as you care for your wife." *A little help would be handy here.*

She stretched out her arm... and hoped.

There was a flap of wings, and a stifled exclamation from her audience followed by muttered exchanges all around the boat as the raven landed, claws digging into her. She didn't flinch. The raven fixed Inge with his gemstone eyes and quorked once, loudly.

"Witch!"

"She's a witch!"

"That's why the wind has gone!"

"She'll be the death of us!"

An explosion of voices, all at once. The boat rocked as some of the fighting men rose to their feet, ready to throw her overboard right there and then. *Hold still,* Helga thought. This was the moment. Out of the corner of her eye she could see Ormar. When he spoke, his voice carried no tension, no threat – just fact.

"Hold your tongues yourselves or I will have them in my hand." As one, the voices died down, but Helga felt the heat of their eyes on her. "She may be a witch, but for the moment she either carries the favour of the gods, which is useful, or she can train a raven, which is impressive." He turned to her. "I will allow her to speak," he said, staring straight at her. "But if I suspect that she is trying to fool us..." He didn't need to say more. The terms had been laid out, and everyone knew.

Let's hope we are right, then.

Helga turned back to Inge. "You care about your name, you care about your kin and I believe if you intended to do it, you would have enjoyed the pleasure of looking him in the eye." The tension drained out of the stocky man like water from a leaky barrel.

She turned to Knut. "You are a survivor. You are smart, tough and underestimated, and it's been like that all your life." The grizzled Viking glared at her, turned his head and spat overboard. "And unlike Inge, I would say you would absolutely stab a sleeping man in the dark."

"And why would I do that, then?" Knut growled.

"Because they annoyed you?" Helga shot back. Out of the corner of her eye she saw smiles on the men, but a lot colder. *I am saying what they think. Let's hope that continues.* "Or because they needed killing? Or maybe, because you could easily imagine that a young upstart could win favour with Ormar – favour that you imagine you deserve but will never get for reasons you will never understand."

"That's a lie!" Knut barked.

"No, it's not," she said. "I can see it in you." She glanced to the side, to confirm her suspicion… *yes.* And Helga smiled. "You have a darkness in you, Knut, and everyone here knows it."

"Did you kill him?" Ormar snapped.

"No!" Knut shouted. "I did not! If I'd gutted that little fish I'd have happily told you all about it."

"And we'd have had the blood price from you, twice over," Skarde growled.

"But I didn't do it!" Knut was half up on his feet, hand on his dagger, ready to defend himself to the death.

All eyes turned to Helga. *Let's play this right.* "He didn't," she said, with finality. "He could have, and would have – but he didn't." Knut slumped back to the side of the boat, muttering to himself and glaring at her. "But Skarde does have a point. The laws say—"

"What do you know of the laws?" Magnus burst out, contemptuously.

Helga turned to him, drained all emotion from her voice, looked him dead in the eye and said,

"Within the gates, ere a man shall go,

Full warily let him watch;

For little he knows where a foe may lurk,

And sit in the seats within."

She fixed the young man with a cold stare. *Do you want to test me?*

He looked away.

She turned to Ormar, and the raven

with her. *Let's hope this one is as smart as he seems.*

"The laws say," she continued, "that the styriman is responsible for his ship and all aboard it on the journey, the mission and the return. Any court in the land would uphold Skarde's demand, and the blood price must be paid. As the boy's kin, Skarde and Inge should receive his share."

Ormar looked at her, frowning. For a moment he seemed frozen in time – but then he spoke. "This has the air of truth about it." He kneeled down, and coins clinked. When he stood up, he held a weighty bag. "Let's get this done with. Come and claim it."

Skarde looked at Inge, who shrugged and gestured for his lanky cousin to move.

Picking his way between planks, bags and weaponry, he moved up to the tiller, where Ormar stood.

"I am right, though, am I not?" Helga said, when the two men were side by side. "You are both his uncles?"

"We are," Skarde said.

"I see. And you are from…"

"Just outside Ribe."

"That's funny!" Helga said, smiling. "I passed through there recently."

"Did you?" Skarde said, hand on the bag.

"I did," Helga said. "Nothing but gossiping fishwives, though. One of them told me she'd heard a story of a woman who got pulled behind the hedge by her husband's foster-brother, who then started whispering that their cousin did the deed. Can you imagine?" There was a moment of absolute silence. "Can you imagine what would have happened if that man's son knew who'd done it? If he'd seen? That would have been something to kill for, wouldn't it?"

"What are you talking about?" Skarde sputtered. "Fishwives' tales! I don't believe—"

He never saw Gisli coming. The rope was looped over him in the blink of an eye, tightened to breath-stopping before he could think to thrash about, and the knife removed from him. The styriman's second in command had inched in behind Skarde, waiting for a signal, and had him tied up in moments. Even if he wanted, the warrior would not have been able to move his arms.

Now Ormar stood before Skarde and looked him dead in the eye. "Tell me she's lying," he said, calmly and kindly. "In fact – tell your brother. Tell your brother that you never touched his wife, that you never lied to his face, that you never blamed your kin." Moving the thin man firmly, he turned him towards Inge, who sat stricken up against the side of the boat, staring open-mouthed.

Skarde blinked, stuttered – and then looked down to his feet.

Ormar looked at Gisli, who gently reclaimed the bag from Skarde's hand. "Inge," he said. "You are owed the blood price for your cousin Trygve. What do you say?"

Inge looked at Ormar, and nodded.

With a simple heave and a dull, deep splash, Skarde went overboard and sank like a stone.

"He deserved no better, and shall not reach Valhalla. He had no honour, and will be food for the fishes." Ormar looked at Helga. "You're useful," he said. "You'll stick around."

"Not as if I have anywhere else to go," Helga said, daring a half-smile.

Ormar glanced pointedly at the place where Skarde had disappeared, then smiled back. "Sails!" he barked.

The raven quorked in mimicry.

The moment the boom clanked into place a wind came blowing from the east, billowing and filling the sails.

Helga sat down next to Breki.

"Have you ever been to Ribe?" the young wrestler said.

"No," Helga said. "The story was in his face, in the way he looked when he thought the blame was shifting. He thought if he did it and kept his mouth shut, they'd eventually blame the one who couldn't defend himself. But he wasn't as smart as he thought he was." The raven cocked its head and looked at Helga, a twinkle in its eye. She leaned back against the side of the ship and enjoyed the wind in her hair, listening to the hiss of the waves and the snap of the cloth.

"They rarely are."

About the Author

Snorri Kristjansson is an Icelandic teacher and writer, currently residing in Edinburgh with his wife and son.

His works include *The Valhalla Saga* and *The Helga Finnsdottir Mysteries*.

He is an avid chess player and a chocolate fiend.

Also by Snorri Kristjansson

THE HELGA FINNSDOTTIR
MYSTERIES

Kin

Council

THE VALHALLA SAGA

Swords of Good Men

Blood Will Follow

Path of Gods

More dyslexic friendly

titles coming soon...

BOTH
PUBLISHING

Lightning Source UK Ltd.
Milton Keynes UK
UKHW011812100922
408646UK00001B/57